# THE ETERNAL HOUSE

WENDY SHEFFIELD

*Spiritwriterspeaks*

Previous publications by Wendy Sheffield include:

## Non Fiction
Spirit Writer (Books 1-4) A Journey of Spiritual
Awakening and Self-Discovery
Which encompasses
Spirit Writer: The Beginning (Book 1)
Pure Spirit: Spiritual Inspiration For All (Book 2)
Spirit Healer: Healing Past, Present and Future
(Book 3)
The Final Awakening: I Am A Healer! (Book 4)

The Devil Within: Evil In This World Today
Spirit Writer: This Journey Called Life
Spirit Writer: The Spirit Guide Connection
Spirit Writer: Exploring the Enigma of the Spirit World

## Fiction
Whispers from the Shadows: Tales of Light and
Darkness
The Magical Guardians: Discover Your Inner Light
Beyond Time: Love Has No Boundaries
Spooky Tales for Little Monsters

To my spirit guides who are forever by my side...

"Believe in the power of light, for it has the ability to illuminate even the darkest corners of our world, dispelling fear, doubt, and despair."

# Contents

# Introduction

**PART ONE: THE EXTERNAL HOUSE**

In the chilling pages of "The Eternal House," readers will be transported into a world of darkness and despair. This horror book follows the harrowing journey of John and Emily, a couple in search of their dream home. Little do they know, their quest will lead them to a house that holds a sinister secret.

"The Eternal House" is a spine-tingling tale that will leave readers questioning the boundaries between the living and the dead, and the power of redemption in the face of eternal torment.

**PART TWO: BONUS CONTENT**

This contains a selection of short horror stories linked in with the main story.

**1. Short Story: "Whispers in the Night"**

# Part 1
# THE ETERNAL HOUSE

# Chapter 1

## The Beginning

John and Emily had been searching for their dream home for months. They had scoured countless listings, visited numerous properties, but nothing seemed to capture their hearts. That was until they stumbled upon a listing for a house that seemed too good to be true.

The moment they laid eyes on the house, they were captivated by its beauty. It stood tall and majestic, surrounded by a lush garden that seemed to whisper secrets. The exterior was adorned with intricate details, and the large windows invited sunlight to dance within its walls. It was a house straight out of their dreams.

As they approached the front door, a chill ran down their spines. The air seemed heavy, and a sense of unease settled upon them. But they brushed it off as mere nerves, attributing it to the excitement of finally finding their perfect home.

John reached out and turned the doorknob, and the door creaked open, revealing a grand foyer. The couple stepped inside, their eyes widening in awe. The interior was just as breathtaking as the exterior. The walls were adorned with elegant wallpaper, and the hardwood floors gleamed under the soft glow of the chandelier.

But there was something off about the house. It felt as if it held a secret, a hidden darkness lurking beneath its beauty. Emily couldn't shake the feeling that they were being watched, that unseen eyes were observing their every move.

John, always the practical one, tried to dismiss Emily's unease. "It's just an old house, Em," he said, trying to reassure her. "We've been looking for so long, and this is the closest we've come to finding our dream home. Let's give it a chance."

Reluctantly, Emily nodded, pushing aside her apprehensions. They continued exploring the house, moving from room to room, envisioning their future within its walls. Each room held its own charm, but there was an underlying sense of melancholy that they couldn't ignore.

As they reached the top of the grand staircase, Emily's eyes were drawn to a portrait hanging on the wall. It depicted a family, their smiles frozen in time. The couple in the portrait bore a striking resemblance to John and Emily, sending a shiver down their spines.

"John, look," Emily whispered, pointing at the portrait. "They look just like us."

John's eyes widened as he studied the portrait. It was as if they were looking into a mirror, but the couple in the painting seemed haunted, their eyes filled with sorrow. It was a chilling resemblance that left them both speechless.

Unnerved, they decided to leave the house and gather their thoughts. As they stepped outside, the heavy feeling that had settled upon them lifted, and they took in deep breaths of fresh air. They exchanged a glance, silently acknowledging the strange energy that permeated the house.

Driving away, John and Emily couldn't help but feel a pull towards the house, as if it was calling out to them, beckoning them to return. They knew deep down that their search for a dream home had come to an end, but they also knew that the journey ahead would be filled with more than they could have ever imagined.

Little did they know that the beautiful but eerie house held a secret that would forever change their lives. Their journey into the depths of the eternal house was about to begin, and they would soon discover that their dream home was anything but a sanctuary. It was a place where their lives would be forever entwined with the darkness that resided within its walls.

## Chapter 2
# The Purchase

John and Emily couldn't shake off the allure of the eternal house. Despite the unsettling feeling they experienced during their initial visit, they found themselves drawn back to its enchanting presence. The house seemed to have cast a spell on them, and they couldn't resist its pull.

After careful consideration and discussions, John and Emily made the life-altering decision to purchase the eternal house. They were willing to overlook the strange occurrences and the eerie atmosphere in exchange for the chance to call this magnificent place their home.

Unaware of the dark secret that lay hidden within the house's walls, they eagerly contacted the real estate agent to proceed with the purchase. The paperwork was swiftly completed, and the keys to the eternal house were handed over to John and Emily.

Excitement and anticipation filled their hearts as they stepped foot into their new home. They were determined to create a haven within the house's mysterious confines, oblivious to the challenges that awaited them.

As they settled into their new abode, John and Emily couldn't help but notice the absence of the previous owners. It was customary for the sellers to provide a warm welcome or at least some guidance during the transition, but there was no sign of them. It was as if they had vanished into thin air.

Curiosity gnawed at John and Emily, prompting them to enquire about the previous owners. They reached out to the real estate agent, hoping to gather some information. To their surprise, the agent seemed hesitant to discuss the previous owners, offering vague responses and quickly changing the subject.

Undeterred, John and Emily decided to take matters into their own hands. They scoured public records, local archives, and even reached out to neighbours in an attempt to uncover the truth. However, their efforts yielded little information. It was as if the previous owners had intentionally erased their existence.

One day, while exploring the attic, John stumbled upon a dusty box hidden beneath a pile of old books. Intrigued, he opened it, revealing a collection of photographs and personal belongings. Among the items was a journal, its pages yellowed with age.

As John flipped through the journal, he discovered entries written by the previous owners. The words painted a picture of despair, loneliness, and a growing sense of entrapment within the eternal house. The more he read, the more he realized that the previous owners had experienced the same eerie occurrences and unexplained phenomena that John and Emily were now facing.

Determined to find answers, John and Emily decided to track down the previous owners themselves. They managed to locate an address and paid them a visit, hoping to gain insight into the house's dark secret.

To their surprise, the previous owners seemed strangely detached and distant. Their eyes held a haunted look, and their voices trembled as they spoke. They warned John and Emily to leave the eternal house, to escape its clutches before it was too late. But they couldn't provide a clear explanation or a solution to the mysterious happenings.

Confused and unsettled, John and Emily left the meeting with more questions than answers. The encounter only deepened their determination to uncover the truth behind the eternal house's dark secret. They were now more aware than ever that their lives were intertwined with a history they couldn't comprehend.

Little did they know that their journey into the depths of the eternal house was far from over. The previous owners' warning echoed in their minds, fueling their determination to unravel the enigma that surrounded their new home. They were about to embark on a path that would test their courage, sanity, and the very essence of their existence.

## Chapter 3
# Settling In

John and Emily stood at the threshold of the eternal house, their excitement palpable as they prepared to embark on a new chapter of their lives. With each step they took inside, the house seemed to welcome them, its walls whispering promises of a peaceful and fulfilling future.

As they began unpacking their belongings, a sense of anticipation filled the air. The rooms slowly transformed, taking on the personal touches that reflected John and Emily's unique tastes and personalities. They worked together, arranging furniture, hanging artwork, and creating a space that felt like home.

But amidst the excitement of settling in, strange occurrences began to unfold. Objects would inexplicably move from one place to another, as if guided by an unseen hand. Lights flickered at odd intervals, casting eerie shadows on the walls. Whispers echoed through the hallways, their origin impossible to pinpoint.

At first, John and Emily dismissed these incidents as mere coincidences. They attributed the moving objects to their own forgetfulness and the flickering lights to faulty wiring. They laughed off the whispers as the wind rustling through the trees outside. It was easier to believe in rational explanations than to acknowledge the growing unease that settled within them.

But as the days turned into weeks, the occurrences became more frequent and harder to ignore. The whispers grew louder, their words indistinguishable yet filled with an undeniable sense of urgency. Shadows danced in the corners of their vision, disappearing when they turned to look. The air grew heavy, as if laden with secrets waiting to be revealed.

Emily couldn't shake the feeling of being watched. She would catch glimpses of movement out of the corner of her eye, only to find nothing there when she turned her head. The sensation of being observed intensified when she was alone in the house, sending shivers down her spine.

John, too, began to experience his own share of unsettling events. He would wake up in the middle of the night, drenched in sweat, unable to recall the nightmares that plagued his sleep. The temperature in certain rooms would inexplicably drop, causing him to shiver despite the warmth of the season.

Despite these disturbances, John and Emily tried to maintain a sense of normalcy. They carried on with their daily routines, hoping that the strange occurrences would eventually fade away. They convinced themselves that it was just their imagination playing tricks on them, that the house was simply settling into its new inhabitants.

But deep down, they couldn't shake the growing unease that gnawed at their souls. They began to question their decision to purchase the eternal house, wondering if they had unknowingly stepped into a nightmare rather than their dream home.

As the days turned into nights, and the nights into weeks, John and Emily's dismissal of the strange occurrences began to waver. The line between reality and the supernatural blurred, and they found themselves teetering on the edge of a truth they were not yet ready to face.

Little did they know that the house held secrets far darker than they could have ever imagined. The strange occurrences were not mere coincidences but the first whispers of a haunting that would consume their lives. The eternal house had awakened, and it was determined to reveal its true nature to its unsuspecting inhabitants.

In the depths of the night, as John and Emily lay in bed, the whispers grew louder, their words finally reaching their ears. The time for denial was coming to an end, and the couple would soon be forced to confront the chilling reality that awaited them within the walls of the eternal house.

## Chapter 4
# Trapped Within

John and Emily's unease grew into a suffocating fear as they realized that something was terribly wrong within the eternal house. Their attempts to leave the house were met with an inexplicable force that held them captive, no matter how hard they tried to escape.

It started innocently enough. John would reach for the doorknob, only to find it frozen in place, refusing to budge. Emily would push against the windows, but they remained sealed shut, as if fused with an unseen barrier. Panic set in as they realized that they were trapped within the confines of the eternal house.

Frantic, they searched for alternative exits, hoping to find a way out. But to their dismay, every door and window they encountered was mysteriously sealed shut, as if the house itself was determined to keep them imprisoned within its walls.

Their desperation grew as they pounded on the walls, screaming for help, but their cries fell on deaf ears. The house seemed to absorb their pleas, leaving them feeling isolated and abandoned. It was as if the eternal house had become a prison, a place where their freedom was nothing more than an illusion.

As the days turned into weeks, John and Emily's attempts to escape became more desperate. They tried everything they could think of, from breaking down doors to smashing windows, but their efforts were in vain. The house remained steadfast, its grip on them unyielding.

With each failed attempt, their hope dwindled, replaced by a sense of resignation. They were trapped within the eternal house, cut off from the outside world, and at the mercy of the dark forces that held them captive.

In their search for answers, John and Emily delved deeper into the house's history. They discovered that the previous owners had also experienced the same entrapment, their lives forever bound to the eternal house. It became clear that the house itself was a malevolent entity, feeding off the souls of those who dared to enter.

As they explored further, they stumbled upon a hidden room, concealed behind a bookshelf. Inside, they found a collection of old journals, filled with the desperate pleas of previous inhabitants who had fallen victim to the eternal house's curse. The journals spoke of a powerful force that sealed the doors and windows, trapping its victims within its clutches for eternity.

Fear gripped John and Emily's hearts as they realized the true nature of the eternal house. They were not alone in their suffering; countless souls had been ensnared by its dark power. The house had become a prison, a place where time stood still, and their lives were forever suspended.

With each passing day, the house seemed to tighten its grip on them, its malevolence seeping into their very beings. They could feel their own life force draining away, as if the house was feeding off their essence. It became clear that their existence within the eternal house was no longer a matter of choice but a cruel fate they were forced to endure.

Trapped within the eternal house, John and Emily faced a grim reality. They were prisoners in a realm where the boundaries of time and space were distorted, and escape seemed impossible. Their only hope now was to uncover the secrets that bound the house and find a way to break free from its clutches before their own lives were consumed by its insidious power.

As the darkness closed in around them, John and Emily vowed to fight against the eternal house's hold, to reclaim their freedom and restore their shattered lives.

Chapter 5
# The Haunting Begins

Within the confines of the eternal house, a malevolent energy stirred, awakening a haunting that would torment John and Emily. As the days turned into nights, the house came alive with paranormal activity, unleashing a torrent of ghostly apparitions and unsettling voices that echoed through its halls.

It started subtly, with flickering lights and unexplained drafts that sent chills down their spines. But soon, the haunting escalated, and the house became a playground for the supernatural. Shadows danced along the walls, taking on eerie forms that seemed to mock the living. Objects levitated and spun in mid-air, defying the laws of gravity.

John and Emily found themselves face to face with ghostly apparitions, their translucent figures hauntingly beautiful yet filled with an otherworldly sorrow. They would catch glimpses of ethereal figures in the corner of their eyes, only for them to vanish when they turned to look directly at them.

The voices that filled the air were a cacophony of whispers, moans, and anguished cries. They seemed to come from all directions, their words a jumbled mix of pleas, warnings, and unintelligible murmurs. The voices echoed through the house, reverberating in John and Emily's minds, leaving them on edge and questioning their sanity.

Nighttime became the most harrowing for the couple. As they lay in bed, the air would grow heavy, suffocating them with an oppressive presence. The room would fill with an icy chill, and the sound of footsteps would echo through the darkness, drawing closer and closer.

One night, as John and Emily huddled together, seeking solace in each other's presence, they heard a child's laughter. It was a haunting sound, filled with both innocence and malevolence. The laughter echoed through the house, growing louder and more distorted with each passing moment.

They followed the sound, their hearts pounding in their chests, until they reached the attic. The laughter seemed to emanate from within, drawing them closer to the source of the haunting. With trembling hands, they pushed open the attic door, revealing a scene that would forever be etched in their minds.

In the dim light, they saw a child, translucent and ethereal, playing with a long-forgotten toy. The child's eyes held a sadness that pierced their souls, and as they watched, the child slowly faded away, leaving behind an overwhelming sense of loss and despair.

The encounters with the supernatural became more frequent and intense, leaving John and Emily on edge at all times. They could no longer dismiss the haunting as mere coincidence or imagination. The eternal house had become a battleground between the living and the dead, and they were caught in the crossfire.

As the haunting intensified, John and Emily realized that they were not just witnesses to the supernatural, but active participants in a battle for their souls. They were being tested, pushed to the brink of their sanity, as the house sought to claim them as its own.

In the face of the haunting, John and Emily clung to each other, finding strength in their love and determination to survive. They knew that they had to uncover the truth behind the eternal house's dark past, to understand the restless spirits that roamed its halls, if they were to have any hope of breaking free from its clutches.

With each encounter, they delved deeper into the house's history, unearthing tales of tragedy, betrayal, and unfinished business. They sought answers from the ghostly apparitions, hoping to find a way to appease the restless souls and bring peace to the eternal house.

But as they ventured further into the heart of the haunting, they realized that the answers they sought would not come easily. The house had become a labyrinth of secrets, and the spirits within were determined to keep their truths buried.

Undeterred, John and Emily vowed to press on, to face the horrors that awaited them within the eternal house. They would confront the restless spirits that whispered in the darkness, their voices echoing through the empty halls. Armed with only their courage and determination, John and Emily ventured deeper into the labyrinthine corridors, their hearts pounding with anticipation and fear. Each step they took brought them closer to the truth, closer to uncovering the secrets that had plagued the house for centuries. The air grew heavy with an otherworldly presence, as if the spirits themselves were watching, waiting for their arrival. But John and Emily refused to be swayed by the eerie atmosphere. They knew that their mission was greater than their own fears. With every passing moment, their resolve grew stronger, their bond unbreakable. Together, they would face the horrors head-on, determined to bring peace to the restless souls trapped within the eternal house.

# Chapter 6
## The Dark History

Determined to unravel the mysteries that plagued the eternal house, John and Emily delved into the depths of its dark history. They spent countless hours researching the house and its previous owners, hoping to uncover the truth behind the haunting that held them captive.

Their search led them to local archives, old newspaper clippings, and interviews with long-time residents of the area. Slowly, the pieces of the puzzle began to come together, revealing a tragic event that had occurred years ago, resulting in the house's curse.

They discovered that the eternal house had once been a place of joy and happiness, owned by a loving family. The previous owners, the Thompsons, had lived there with their young daughter, Sarah. The house had been their sanctuary, a place where they had built a life filled with laughter and love.

But tragedy struck one fateful night. A fire engulfed the eternal house, consuming it in a blaze of destruction. The Thompsons, trapped within its walls, perished in the inferno, their lives cut short in a moment of unimaginable horror.

The fire had left an indelible mark on the house, its walls forever stained with the sorrow and anguish of that tragic night. The souls of the Thompson family, unable to find peace, became trapped within the eternal house, their presence haunting its every corner.

John and Emily's hearts ached as they uncovered the details of the fire and the Thompsons' untimely demise. They realized that the haunting they experienced was a result of the restless spirits seeking resolution, their souls bound to the eternal house by the weight of their unfinished business.

Driven by compassion and a desire to bring peace to the tormented souls, John and Emily embarked on a mission to uncover the truth behind the Thompsons' tragedy. They sought out surviving relatives, old friends, and anyone who could shed light on the events that had unfolded that fateful night.

Through their relentless pursuit of answers, they discovered a long-kept secret that had been buried beneath layers of silence and guilt. It was revealed that the fire had not been an accident but a deliberate act of arson, fueled by jealousy and greed.

The Thompsons had been targeted by a neighbour, Mr. Reynolds, who coveted their property and the wealth it represented. Consumed by envy, he had set fire to the eternal house, intending to claim it for himself. In his twisted mind, he believed that by destroying the Thompsons, he could take their place and inherit their fortune.

The revelation of Mr. Reynolds' heinous act sent shockwaves through John and Emily. They realized that the curse that held them captive was not just a result of the tragic fire but also the vengeful spirits of the Thompsons, seeking justice for the injustice that had befallen them.

Armed with this newfound knowledge, John and Emily vowed to right the wrongs of the past. They sought out the assistance of paranormal experts, spiritual guides, and even mediums, hoping to find a way to appease the restless spirits and break free from the eternal house's curse.

Together, they conducted séances, performed cleansing rituals, and offered prayers for the souls of the Thompson family. They listened to the voices of the spirits, offering solace and understanding, as they worked tirelessly to bring closure to the tragic events that had unfolded within the eternal house.

As they delved deeper into their mission, the haunting within the house intensified. The spirits grew more restless, their presence more palpable. But John and Emily remained steadfast, their determination unwavering, as they fought against the malevolent forces that sought to deter them. Shadows danced along the walls, whispering sinister secrets and tempting them to abandon their quest. Yet, John and Emily refused to succumb to the darkness that surrounded them. They knew that their purpose was noble, and they would not let fear consume them. With each encounter, they learned to harness their inner strength, channeling it into a shield against the malevolence that threatened to consume them. Their bond grew stronger with every trial they faced, their trust in each other unwavering. Together, they stood as a beacon of hope amidst the chaos, determined to bring peace to the tormented souls and restore harmony to the eternal house.

## Chapter 7
# The Ghostly Residents

John and Emily stood in the dimly lit hallway of the eternal house, their hearts pounding with anticipation. They had reached a critical point in their journey, where they would come face to face with the spirits of the previous owners, the Thompson family, who were trapped within the house.

As they cautiously moved forward, the air grew heavy with an otherworldly presence. A chill ran down their spines as they felt the gaze of unseen eyes upon them. And then, in the flickering light, the apparitions of Mr. and Mrs. Thompson materialized before them.

The spirits of the Thompsons were ethereal and translucent, their faces etched with sorrow and anger. They spoke with voices that carried both pain and determination, revealing the tragic fate that had befallen them.

"We were once a happy family, living in this house," Mrs. Thompson's voice echoed through the hallway. "But our lives were cut short, consumed by the flames that engulfed us."

Mr. Thompson's voice joined in, filled with bitterness. "We were betrayed, our dreams shattered by the greed and jealousy of a neighbour. Now, we are trapped within these walls, seeking justice for the injustice that befell us."

John and Emily listened, their hearts heavy with empathy for the tormented spirits. They understood the depth of their pain and the desire for revenge that fueled their existence within the eternal house.

The Thompsons revealed the extent of their suffering, recounting the moments leading up to their tragic end. They spoke of the fear and confusion that gripped them as the fire raged around them, the desperate attempts to escape the engulfing flames, and the realization that their lives were slipping away.

"We seek revenge," Mrs. Thompson's voice trembled with anger. "We cannot rest until those responsible for our untimely demise face the consequences of their actions."

John and Emily exchanged glances, understanding the weight of the spirits' words. They knew that the only way to bring peace to the eternal house and free themselves from its clutches was to help the Thompsons find the justice they sought.

With determination in their hearts, John and Emily vowed to uncover the truth behind the arson that had claimed the lives of the Thompson family. They would gather evidence, seek out witnesses, and do whatever it took to bring the guilty party to light.

As they delved deeper into their investigation, they discovered a trail of deceit and betrayal that led them to Mr. Reynolds, the neighbour who had set fire to the eternal house. They confronted him, presenting the evidence they had gathered, and demanded that he take responsibility for his actions.

Mr. Reynolds, now an old man burdened with guilt, confessed to his crime. He admitted to his envy and greed, revealing the depths of his depravity. He had thought that by destroying the Thompsons, he could claim their wealth and live a life of luxury.

But his actions had consequences far beyond what he had anticipated. The curse that had befallen the eternal house was not just the result of the tragic fire but also the vengeful spirits seeking justice for their untimely demise.

With the truth exposed, John and Emily returned to the eternal house, ready to confront the spirits once more. They shared the news of Mr. Reynolds' confession, offering the Thompsons the justice they had longed for.

The spirits of the Thompsons, their anger tempered by the knowledge that their revenge had been achieved, began to fade away. Their ethereal forms dissipated, leaving behind a sense of peace and closure.

# Chapter 8
## Descent into Madness

John and Emily's journey within the eternal house had taken a toll on their mental and emotional well-being. The relentless torment from the spirits had pushed them to the brink of their sanity, blurring the lines between reality and the supernatural.

As the days turned into nights, their once vibrant spirits began to wither under the weight of the haunting. They found it increasingly difficult to distinguish between what was real and what was a product of their tortured minds. The boundaries between the physical world and the realm of the spirits became blurred, leaving them in a perpetual state of confusion and fear.

The spirits, no longer content with mere apparitions and whispers, intensified their torment. They played tricks on John and Emily, distorting their perception of reality. Shadows danced and twisted, whispering sinister secrets that echoed through their minds.

Objects moved on their own, defying the laws of nature, leaving them questioning their own sanity.

Sleep became a distant memory as nightmares plagued their nights. They would wake up in cold sweats, their hearts pounding, unable to shake the feeling of being watched by unseen eyes. The spirits invaded their dreams, weaving a tapestry of terror that bled into their waking hours.

The once cozy rooms of the eternal house now felt suffocating, each corner holding a potential threat. Every creak of the floorboards, every gust of wind, sent shivers down their spines. They were constantly on edge, their nerves frayed, as they struggled to maintain a grip on reality.

Their deteriorating mental and emotional state strained their relationship. Arguments erupted over the smallest of things, fueled by the constant stress and fear that enveloped them. They questioned each other's perceptions, their trust eroded by the relentless haunting.

Desperate for respite, John and Emily sought solace in their research, hoping to find a way to break free from the clutches of the eternal house. They consulted experts in the paranormal, delved into ancient texts, and performed rituals in an attempt to appease the spirits.

But their efforts seemed futile, as the haunting only grew stronger. The spirits reveled in their torment, feeding off their fear and confusion. The line between the living and the dead became increasingly blurred, leaving John and Emily trapped in a nightmarish existence.

In their darkest moments, they contemplated leaving the eternal house behind, abandoning their quest for answers. But the spirits, sensing their weakness, intensified their torment, leaving them with no choice but to confront the haunting head-on.

As they faced the spirits, their minds teetering on the edge of madness, John and Emily found a glimmer of strength within themselves. They realized that succumbing to the torment would mean surrendering their lives to the eternal house, forever trapped in its malevolent grip.

With a newfound determination, they fought back against the spirits, refusing to let their minds be consumed by the darkness. They sought refuge in each other's presence, finding solace in their shared experiences and unwavering love.

Slowly, they began to regain their sense of self, their grip on reality strengthening. They learned to distinguish between the supernatural and the physical, to separate the haunting from their own thoughts. The spirits, sensing their resilience, began to lose their hold on John and Emily.

In their triumph over the descent into madness, John and Emily discovered a newfound strength within themselves. They realized that the power of their love and their unwavering spirit could overcome even the darkest of forces.

Armed with this newfound resilience, they continued their relentless pursuit of the truth. The challenges they faced only fueled their determination, as they refused to be deterred by the horrors that awaited them. With each step forward, they unraveled the mysteries that shrouded the eternal house, inching closer to the heart of the darkness. The spirits, sensing their unwavering resolve, grew restless, their attempts to thwart John and Emily becoming more desperate. But the duo remained unyielding, their spirits unbreakable. They drew strength from the knowledge that their mission was not only for themselves, but for all those who had suffered within the confines of the eternal house. With every obstacle they overcame, they grew more resolute, their purpose burning brighter than ever before. Armed with this newfound resilience, they pressed on, ready to face whatever awaited them in their quest for redemption and closure.

Chapter 9

# The Haunting
# Intensifies

The eternal house, once a place of torment and despair, continued to unleash its malevolent power upon John and Emily. The paranormal activity escalated, growing more violent and terrifying with each passing day.

The spirits, fueled by their vengeful rage, sought to break the resolve of John and Emily. They no longer contented themselves with mere apparitions and whispers. Instead, they unleashed a barrage of physical attacks, determined to inflict pain and terror upon the living.

It started with subtle gestures - a gentle push, a tug on their clothes. But soon, the spirits grew bolder, their actions becoming more aggressive. John and Emily found themselves thrown against walls, their bodies bruised and battered by unseen forces.

The once familiar rooms of the eternal house became a battleground, where objects were hurled through the air with a force that defied explanation. Furniture toppled over, shattering glass and splintering wood. The very foundations of the house seemed to tremble under the weight of the supernatural onslaught.

No longer able to distinguish between the living and the dead, John and Emily lived in a constant state of fear. They were haunted by the spirits' relentless pursuit, their every move shadowed by a malevolent presence. Sleep became a distant memory, as nightmares merged with reality, blurring the lines between the physical and the supernatural.

In their waking hours, they were tormented by the spirits' relentless attacks. Scratches appeared on their bodies, deep and painful, as if inflicted by invisible claws. They were thrown to the ground, their limbs twisted and contorted in unnatural ways. The spirits reveled in their pain, their laughter echoing through the house.

But amidst the chaos and terror, John and Emily refused to surrender. They clung to each other, finding strength in their love and determination to survive. They fought back against the vengeful spirits, their resilience shining through the darkness.

Armed with their knowledge of the house's dark history, they sought out ways to protect themselves. They enlisted the help of spiritual guides and paranormal experts, who provided them with talismans and rituals to ward off the malevolent forces.

With each passing day, their defences grew stronger, their understanding of the supernatural deepening. They learned to anticipate the spirits' attacks, to shield themselves from their wrath. The vengeful entities, sensing their growing strength, became more desperate in their attempts to break their resolve.

One night, as John and Emily huddled together, seeking solace in their shared bravery, the spirits launched their most vicious attack yet. They were surrounded by a whirlwind of fury, as objects flew through the air with a ferocity that threatened to engulf them.

In the midst of the chaos, John and Emily fought back, their voices raised in defiance. They called upon the spirits to reveal themselves, to face the consequences of their actions. And in that moment, the house fell silent.

The spirits, momentarily stunned by the couple's unwavering courage, retreated into the shadows. The eternal house, once a place of torment, seemed to hold its breath, as if acknowledging the indomitable spirit of John and Emily.

Though the haunting had intensified, John and Emily refused to be broken. They knew that their journey was far from over, that they still had much to uncover and resolve within the eternal house. With renewed determination, they prepared themselves for the battles that lay ahead, ready to face the vengeful spirits head-on.

# Chapter 10
## Seeking Help

John and Emily, determined to rid the eternal house of its malevolent spirits, reached out to paranormal experts and spiritualists for assistance. They knew that they couldn't face the haunting alone and needed the expertise of those who understood the supernatural realm.

Through their research, they discovered a network of paranormal investigators and spiritualists who specialized in dealing with hauntings and malevolent entities. They contacted several of them, seeking their guidance and expertise in their battle against the vengeful spirits.

One of the paranormal experts they reached out to was a renowned investigator named Sarah Thompson. Sarah had dedicated her life to studying and understanding the paranormal, and she had a reputation for successfully dealing with even the most challenging cases.

Sarah agreed to visit the eternal house and assess the situation. She arrived with a team of experienced investigators, armed with various tools and techniques to communicate with the spirits and perform necessary rituals.

Together, John, Emily, and the paranormal experts embarked on a journey to cleanse the house of its malevolent presence. They conducted thorough investigations, using EVP (Electronic Voice Phenomenon) recorders, EMF (Electromagnetic Field) detectors, and infrared cameras to capture any evidence of paranormal activity.

As they explored the house, they encountered chilling manifestations of the spirits' presence. Cold spots, disembodied voices, and unexplained phenomena became more apparent. The spirits seemed to grow agitated, their presence intensifying as the investigators delved deeper into their realm.

Sarah and her team worked tirelessly to communicate with the spirits, seeking to understand their grievances and find a way to bring them peace. They performed various rituals and exorcisms, calling upon higher powers to assist in the cleansing process.

The rituals ranged from smudging the house with sacred herbs to conducting séances and prayers. Each attempt was met with mixed results, as the spirits resisted their efforts, their anger and resentment palpable.

Undeterred, the team persisted, their determination unwavering. They sought guidance from spiritualists who specialized in communicating with the spirit world, hoping to gain insight into the spirits' motivations and find a way to resolve their grievances.

Through their combined efforts, they managed to make progress. The malevolent spirits, though still present, began to show signs of weakening. Their attacks became less frequent and less intense as John and Emily's determination and resilience continued to grow. The spirits, once formidable and relentless, now seemed to falter in the face of their unwavering resolve. The duo's unwavering pursuit of the truth and their unwavering bond began to chip away at the malevolence that had plagued the eternal house for so long. With each victory, the spirits' power diminished, their presence becoming more feeble and fleeting. John and Emily could sense the shift in the atmosphere, a glimmer of hope amidst the darkness. They knew that their efforts were not in vain, that their relentless pursuit was making a difference. Encouraged by the signs of weakening, they pressed on with renewed determination, ready to face the final battle against the malevolent spirits and bring an end to the haunting that had tormented the eternal house for far too long.

Chapter 11
# Uncovering the Truth

As John and Emily delved deeper into their investigation of the eternal house, they uncovered the full extent of the curse that had plagued it for generations. They discovered a dark secret that connected their own lives to the malevolent spirits and the haunting that had consumed the house.

Through their research and conversations with spiritualists, they learned that the curse originated from a tragic event that occurred many years ago. The original owners of the house, the Montgomery family, had been victims of a terrible crime. Their lives were cut short, and their souls were trapped within the eternal house, seeking justice and revenge.

John and Emily realized that their own existence was intricately tied to the curse. They were descendants of the Montgomery family, and their presence in the eternal house had awakened the spirits and intensified the haunting. The spirits saw in them a chance for redemption and release from their eternal torment.

The couple understood that breaking the cycle of the curse was the key to their escape. They had to uncover the truth behind the tragic event that had befallen the Montgomery family and find a way to bring justice to their ancestors.

With renewed determination, John and Emily embarked on a quest to uncover the truth. They delved into historical records, interviewed elderly residents of the town, and sought out any information that could shed light on the events that had led to the curse.

Their investigation led them to a long-forgotten diary, hidden away in the attic of the eternal house. The diary belonged to a former resident, who had witnessed the tragic event that had set the curse in motion. Its pages revealed a tale of betrayal, greed, and a desperate act of violence that had forever changed the lives of the Montgomery family.

Armed with this newfound knowledge, John and Emily confronted the spirits once more. They shared the truth they had uncovered, offering the spirits a chance for justice and closure. They pleaded with the vengeful entities to release them from the eternal house, to break the cycle of torment and allow their souls to find peace.

The spirits, their anger tempered by the revelation of the truth, hesitated. They realized that their revenge had been misplaced, that their torment had only perpetuated the cycle of suffering. In that moment, a sense of understanding and forgiveness filled the air.

With a final act of redemption, the spirits relinquished their hold on John and Emily. The eternal house, once a place of darkness and despair, began to fade away, its malevolent presence dissipating into the ether.

John and Emily, free from the clutches of the curse, stood outside the remnants of the eternal house. They looked upon the ruins, a mixture of relief and sadness in their hearts. They had broken the cycle, but they knew that the house would forever hold the memories of the tragic events that had unfolded within its walls.

As they walked away from the remnants of the eternal house, John and Emily carried with them the lessons learned from their harrowing experience. They understood the power of forgiveness, the importance of seeking truth, and the strength of their love in overcoming even the darkest of forces.

Their lives forever changed, they vowed to honour the memory of the Montgomery family and ensure that their tragic tale would never be forgotten. And as they moved forward, they carried with them the knowledge that they had escaped the clutches of the eternal house, forever breaking free from its haunting grip.

Chapter 12
# Confronting the Spirits

The time had come for John and Emily to confront the spirits in a final showdown within the eternal house. They knew that in order to free themselves from its clutches, they had to find a way to release the trapped souls and bring an end to the haunting that had plagued the house for generations.

Armed with the knowledge they had gathered and the strength they had gained throughout their journey, John and Emily entered the eternal house one last time. The air was heavy with anticipation as they made their way through the familiar corridors, their hearts filled with a mixture of determination and trep-idation.

As they reached the heart of the house, they found themselves in a room that seemed to pulsate with an otherworldly energy. The spirits, sensing their pres-ence, materialized before them, their ethereal forms flickering in the dim light.

With unwavering resolve, John and Emily addressed the spirits, speaking words of understanding and empathy. They acknowledged the pain and suffering the spirits had endured, recognizing the injustice that had trapped them within the eternal house.

In a moment of profound connection, John and Emily shared their own experiences, their own struggles, and their desire for freedom. They pleaded with the spirits to release their hold on the house, to find peace and move on to the afterlife.

The spirits, their anger and resentment slowly giving way to a glimmer of hope, listened to John and Emily's words. They realized that their revenge had only perpetuated their own suffering, and that by holding onto their pain, they were trapped in a never-ending cycle of torment.

Together, John and Emily devised a plan to release the trapped souls. They gathered sacred objects and performed a ritual, calling upon higher powers to guide the spirits towards the light. They created a bridge between the physical world and the spiritual realm, offering the spirits a path to redemption and release.

As the ritual unfolded, the energy within the eternal house shifted. The spirits, their ethereal forms glowing with a newfound light, began to ascend towards the heavens. Their anguished cries transformed into whispers of gratitude and forgiveness, echoing through the house one last time.

With each spirit that found release, the weight of the haunting lifted. The eternal house, once a place of darkness and despair, began to transform. The walls seemed to breathe with newfound life, and the air became infused with a sense of peace and tranquility.

John and Emily, their hearts filled with a mixture of relief and sadness, watched as the last of the spirits disappeared into the light. The eternal house, now cleansed of its malevolent presence, stood as a testament to their triumph over darkness.

As they stepped out of the eternal house for the final time, John and Emily felt a sense of liberation wash over them. They had confronted the spirits, found a way to release the trapped souls, and freed themselves from the clutches of the haunting.

Their journey had been arduous, filled with fear and uncertainty, but they emerged stronger and wiser. They carried with them the lessons learned from their encounter with the supernatural, forever changed by their experiences within the eternal house.

As they walked away from the house, hand in hand, John and Emily knew that they had not only freed themselves but also brought peace to the souls that had long been trapped within its walls. They vowed to honour the memory of the spirits and the lessons they had learned, cherishing the newfound freedom they had fought so hard to attain.

And as they looked back one last time, the eternal house stood as a testament to their courage and resilience, a reminder that even in the face of darkness, love and determination could conquer all.

## Chapter 13
# Sacrifice and Redemption

In the final chapter of their harrowing journey, John and Emily faced a pivotal moment within the eternal house. They knew that breaking the curse required a sacrificial decision, one that would test their love, strength, and resolve to the utmost.

As they stood in the heart of the house, surrounded by the lingering presence of the spirits, John and Emily shared a solemn gaze. They understood that their connection to the curse ran deep, and breaking free from the house's grip would demand a great sacrifice.

With heavy hearts, they made the decision to offer themselves as vessels for the spirits' redemption. They believed that by willingly taking on the burden of the curse, they could release the trapped souls and bring an end to the haunting that had plagued the eternal house for generations.

As they prepared for the sacrificial ritual, John and Emily felt a mixture of fear and determination. They knew that their decision would forever alter their lives, but they were willing to make the ultimate sacrifice for the greater good.

With the guidance of spiritualists and the knowledge they had gained throughout their journey, they performed the ritual. They channeled their love and compassion, offering themselves as conduits for the spirits' release.

In a moment of profound connection, the spirits entered John and Emily, their ethereal presence merging with their physical beings. The weight of the curse settled upon them, their bodies trembling under its immense power.

As the spirits inhabited their souls, John and Emily felt a surge of energy and understanding. They saw the world through the eyes of the trapped souls, experiencing their pain, their longing for justice, and their desperate need for redemption.

With each passing moment, the spirits' presence within John and Emily grew stronger. They could hear their voices, feel their emotions, and understand their stories. The couple realized that their sacrifice was not only about breaking the curse but also about finding redemption and closure for the spirits and themselves.

In a final act of courage, John and Emily summoned the strength to release the spirits. They called upon the higher powers they had encountered throughout their journey, asking for guidance and assistance in setting the trapped souls free.

As they uttered the words of release, a brilliant light filled the eternal house. The spirits, their ethereal forms glowing with newfound energy, began to ascend towards the heavens. Their cries of anguish transformed into whispers of gratitude and forgiveness, echoing through the house one last time.

With each spirit that found release, the weight of the curse lifted from John and Emily. They felt a sense of liberation and closure wash over them, their souls finally free from the grip of the eternal house.

As the last spirit disappeared into the light, John and Emily collapsed to the ground, physically and emotionally drained. They had made the ultimate sacrifice, but they had also found redemption and closure within the walls of the eternal house.

As they lay there, hand in hand, they felt a profound sense of peace and fulfilment. They had broken the curse, released the trapped souls, and found their own redemption in the process. The sacrifices they had made were not in vain, for they had brought an end to the haunting that had plagued the eternal house for generations.

As they emerged from the house, John and Emily carried with them the lessons learned from their journey. They understood the power of sacrifice, the importance of empathy and forgiveness, and the strength of their love in overcoming even the darkest of forces.

Their lives forever changed, they walked away from the eternal house, leaving behind a legacy of courage and redemption. They knew that their sacrifice would be remembered, and the spirits they had set free would find eternal peace.

And as they looked back one last time, the eternal house stood as a testament to their sacrifice and the triumph of love over darkness. They had found redemption and closure, forever breaking free from the house's grip and embracing a future filled with hope and possibility.

## Chapter 14

# Escaping the Nightmare

In the aftermath of their sacrificial decision and the release of the trapped spirits, John and Emily found themselves standing outside the eternal house, their hearts filled with a mixture of relief and exhaustion. They had managed to escape the clutches of the house's haunting grip, forever changed by their harrowing experience.

As they looked back at the once-menacing structure, they felt a sense of liberation wash over them. The eternal house, once a place of darkness and despair, now stood as a testament to their triumph over the supernatural forces that had plagued them for so long.

With each step they took away from the cursed property, John and Emily felt a weight lifting from their shoulders. They had endured unimaginable horrors, faced their deepest fears, and emerged stronger and wiser on the other side.

As they walked hand in hand, they couldn't help but reflect on the lessons they had learned throughout their journey. They understood the power of resilience, the importance of trust and communication, and the strength of their love in overcoming even the most nightmarish of situations.

The experience had forever changed their perspective on life. They no longer took their existence for granted, realizing the fragility of their own mortality and the preciousness of every moment. They vowed to live each day to the fullest, cherishing the simple joys and embracing the beauty of the world around them.

Though scarred by their encounter with the supernatural, John and Emily found solace in the fact that they had not only escaped the nightmare but also brought peace to the trapped souls that had long been tormented within the eternal house. Their sacrifice had not been in vain, and they carried the memory of the spirits with them, forever grateful for the lessons they had taught them.

As they left the cursed property behind, John and Emily knew that their lives would never be the same. They had faced their deepest fears, confronted the darkest of forces, and emerged as survivors. The experience had forged an unbreakable bond between them, one that would carry them through any future challenges they may face.

They also understood the importance of sharing their story, of shedding light on the supernatural realm and the power it holds over those who dare to enter its domain. They vowed to use their experience to help others, to offer guidance and support to those who may find themselves trapped in similar nightmares.

As they walked away from the eternal house, John and Emily carried with them a newfound sense of purpose. They had escaped the clutches of the supernatural, forever changed by their harrowing experience. And as they looked towards the future, they did so with hope, resilience, and a deep appreciation for the light that had emerged from the darkness.

## Chapter 15
# **Rebuilding their Lives**

After escaping the clutches of the eternal house, John and Emily found themselves faced with the daunting task of rebuilding their lives. Though physically free from its haunting grip, they were haunted by the memories of the horrors they had endured within its walls.

As they settled into their new normal, they realized that the impact of their harrowing experience ran deep. The nightmares and flashbacks of the eternal house lingered, casting a shadow over their daily lives. They knew that in order to truly move forward, they needed to confront and heal from the trauma they had endured.

With a shared determination, John and Emily sought therapy to help them navigate the emotional aftermath of their ordeal. They found solace in the presence of a compassionate therapist who guided them through the process of healing. Through therapy, they learned coping mechanisms to manage their anxiety and nightmares, and they began to slowly unravel the layers of trauma that had been inflicted upon them.

In the safety of the therapy room, John and Emily shared their deepest fears and vulnerabilities. They spoke of the lingering sense of dread that followed them, the moments of paralyzing fear that would grip their hearts, and the overwhelming sadness that washed over them when they thought of the eternal house.

Their therapist provided them with tools to process their emotions and encouraged them to lean on each other for support. Together, they created a safe space within their relationship where they could openly discuss their experiences and provide comfort to one another.

As time passed, John and Emily began to see progress in their healing journey. The nightmares became less frequent, and the memories of the eternal house no longer held the same power over them. They discovered strength within themselves and within their relationship, finding solace in the fact that they had faced their darkest fears and emerged stronger on the other side.

Outside of therapy, John and Emily focused on rebuilding their lives. They surrounded themselves with loved ones who offered understanding and support. They engaged in activities that brought them joy and helped them reconnect with the beauty of the world around them.

They also found solace in giving back to their community. They shared their story with others who had experienced trauma, offering a listening ear and words of encouragement. Through their own healing journey, they discovered a newfound empathy and a desire to help others find their own path to recovery.

As the days turned into weeks and the weeks into months, John and Emily continued to rebuild their lives. The memories of the eternal house would always be a part of them, but they no longer defined their existence. They had faced their demons head-on and emerged as survivors, forever changed but resilient in their pursuit of happiness and peace.

And as they looked towards the future, John and Emily knew that their journey was far from over. They understood that healing was a lifelong process, one that required patience, self-compassion, and a commitment to their own well-being. But they also knew that they had each other, a love that had withstood the darkest of trials, and together, they would continue to rebuild their lives, finding strength and solace in the light that had emerged from the darkness of the eternal house.

## Chapter 16
# The Legacy Lives On

Years had passed since John and Emily had escaped the clutches of the eternal house. They had rebuilt their lives, found healing, and moved forward, but the memory of their harrowing experience remained etched in their minds. They had hoped that their sacrifice and the release of the trapped spirits would bring an end to the haunting, but they soon discovered that the dark secret of the eternal house continued to live on.

The house stood abandoned, its once-grand facade now weathered and worn. Potential buyers were drawn to its eerie allure, unaware of the horrors that lay within its walls. The dark secret of the eternal house remained hidden, waiting to ensnare those who dared to enter.

As the years went by, the cycle of trapped souls and eternal torment continued. The house seemed to have a magnetic pull, drawing in unsuspecting victims who were unaware of the malevolent force that awaited them. The spirits, unable to find peace, perpetuated the haunting, their anguished cries echoing through the empty halls.

John and Emily, burdened by the knowledge of the ongoing torment, felt a sense of responsibility. They knew that they had to warn others, to prevent more innocent lives from falling victim to the eternal house's curse. They shared their story, reaching out to local authorities, paranormal investigators, and anyone who would listen, hoping to shed light on the dark secret that lay within the abandoned property.

But their warnings often fell on deaf ears. The allure of the eternal house was too strong for some, and they dismissed the tales as mere superstition. The cycle of trapped souls and eternal torment continued, as the house claimed new victims, forever adding to its dark legacy.

John and Emily, unable to shake the weight of their knowledge, continued their efforts to bring awareness to the haunting. They documented their experiences, sharing their story through books, documentaries, and online platforms. They hoped that by shining a light on the eternal house's dark secret, they could save others from the same fate they had endured.

But despite their best efforts, the legacy of the eternal house lived on. The cycle of trapped souls and eternal torment continued, a reminder of the darkness that lurked within its walls. The house remained a haunting reminder of the power of the supernatural, a cautionary tale for those who dared to venture into the unknown.

As John and Emily looked upon the abandoned house, they couldn't help but feel a sense of sadness and frustration. They had hoped that their sacrifice and the release of the trapped spirits would bring an end to the haunting, but the eternal house remained a beacon of darkness, forever ensnaring those who dared to enter.

And so, the legacy of the eternal house lived on, a chilling reminder of the consequences of unchecked supernatural forces. John and Emily vowed to continue their efforts, to warn others and shed light on the dark secret that lay within the abandoned property. They hoped that one day, their message would be heard, and the cycle of trapped souls and eternal torment would finally come to an end.

## Chapter 17
# **Epilogue**

Years had passed since the events that unfolded within the eternal house. The world had moved on, but the house remained, standing as a foreboding presence in the quiet town. Its dark history had become the stuff of legends, whispered among locals and passed down through generations.

As the years went by, the house stood as a silent witness to the passage of time. Its once-grand architecture had succumbed to decay, its windows shattered, and its walls covered in ivy. But despite its dilapidated state, the house still exuded an eerie aura, a reminder of the horrors that had unfolded within its walls.

Hints of its dark history continued to linger, like whispers carried on the wind. Locals spoke of strange occurrences, of unexplained noises and fleeting glimpses of shadowy figures. Some claimed to have seen the spirits of the trapped souls, forever bound to the eternal house, their anguished cries echoing through the night.

The legends surrounding the house grew, attracting thrill-seekers and paranormal enthusiasts from far and wide. They came in search of answers, hoping to uncover the truth behind the haunting. But the house remained elusive, its secrets guarded by an unseen force.

As the years turned into decades, the potential for a sequel loomed in the air. The eternal house, with its dark history and lingering presence, left room for new stories to be told. The possibility of uncovering more about the supernatural forces that resided within its walls enticed both curious minds and those seeking a thrill.

Authors and filmmakers were drawn to the house's allure, weaving tales of horror and suspense inspired by its dark legacy. The eternal house became a symbol of the unknown, a canvas upon which new nightmares could be painted.

And so, the story of the eternal house continued to captivate the imaginations of those who dared to delve into its mysteries. The potential for a sequel, with its promise of uncovering more secrets and delving deeper into the supernatural realm, remained a tantalizing prospect.

But as the years passed, the eternal house stood as a reminder that some secrets are meant to remain hidden. Its dark history and the trapped souls within its walls served as a cautionary tale, a reminder of the consequences of delving too deeply into the unknown.

And so, the house remained, a silent sentinel in the town's landscape, its presence forever etched in the memories of those who had encountered its horrors. The potential for a sequel lingered, leaving room for new stories to be told, but the true nature of the eternal house would always remain a mystery, its secrets locked away within its decaying walls.

# Part 2
# BONUS CONTENT

Welcome to the bonus content of "The Eternal House." In this section, we delve deeper into the haunting and its impact on the lives of other characters who have encountered the malevolent force within its walls. Through short stories and interviews, we gain additional insights into the horrors that unfolded and the lasting effects they had on those involved.

These bonus stories and interviews offer a glimpse into the wider impact of the eternal house, showcasing the diverse experiences and perspectives of those affected by its haunting. They provide additional layers to the narrative, deepening our understanding of the supernatural forces at play and the profound effects they have on the lives they touch.

As you explore these bonus contents, may they further immerse you in the chilling world of "The Eternal

House" and leave you contemplating the enduring power of the supernatural and its impact on the human spirit.

**1. Short Story: "Whispers in the Night"**

**2. Interview: The Paranormal Investigator**

**3. Short Story: "The Lost Journal"**

**4. Interview: The Local Historian**

Chapter 1

# Short Story: "Whispers in the Night"

In this short story, we follow Sarah, a young woman who unknowingly purchases a painting from an estate sale that once hung within the eternal house. As the painting finds its way into her home, Sarah begins to experience strange occurrences, hearing whispers in the night and feeling an unexplainable presence. Will she uncover the connection between the painting and the eternal house before it's too late?

Once upon a time, in a quaint little town, there lived a young woman named Sarah. She had always been drawn to the mysterious and the unknown, finding solace in the stories of haunted houses and paranormal encounters. Little did she know that her own life was about to take a chilling turn.

One sunny afternoon, Sarah stumbled upon an estate sale while exploring the town. Among the various items on display, a painting caught her eye. It was a beautiful landscape, depicting a serene countryside bathed in the warm hues of sunset. Intrigued by its beauty, Sarah decided to purchase the painting and bring it home.

As the painting found its place on the wall of her cozy living room, Sarah couldn't help but feel a strange energy emanating from it. She dismissed it as her overactive imagination, attributing the feeling to her fascination with the supernatural. Little did she know that the painting had a dark secret, one that would soon unravel before her very eyes.

That night, as Sarah lay in bed, she began to hear faint whispers in the stillness of the night. At first, she thought it was just the wind outside or her mind playing tricks on her. But the whispers grew louder and more distinct, as if someone was trying to communicate with her.

Curiosity mingled with fear, Sarah followed the whispers, which seemed to lead her back to the painting. She stared at it intently, her heart pounding in her chest. Suddenly, the painting seemed to come alive, the colours shifting and swirling before her eyes. Sarah gasped in disbelief.

The whispers grew louder, and Sarah could make out fragments of words and phrases. They spoke of sorrow, trapped souls, and the eternal house. It sent shivers down her spine, as if the spirits of the eternal house were reaching out to her through the painting.

Determined to uncover the truth, Sarah delved into research about the eternal house. She discovered its dark history, the tales of restless spirits and unexplained phenomena that had plagued its inhabitants for centuries. And then, she stumbled upon a photograph that sent chills down her spine - the painting she had purchased was once hung within the walls of the eternal house.

Realizing the connection between the painting and the whispers, Sarah knew she had to confront the spirits and bring them peace. She sought the help of a renowned paranormal investigator, who guided her through a series of rituals and ceremonies to communicate with the trapped souls.

As Sarah stood before the painting, she addressed the spirits with compassion and understanding. She acknowledged their pain and offered them a chance at redemption. The room grew still, and the whispers ceased. The painting returned to its serene state, as if the spirits had finally found solace.

In the days that followed, Sarah felt a sense of peace and tranquility in her home. The whispers in the night were replaced with a comforting silence. The connection between the painting and the eternal house had been severed, and the spirits had found their release.

Sarah's experience with the painting had forever changed her. She became an advocate for those who had encountered the supernatural, sharing her story and offering support to those in need. The painting, once a source of mystery and fear, became a symbol of resilience and the power of compassion.

And as Sarah looked at the painting, now hanging on her wall, she couldn't help but feel a sense of gratitude. It had led her on a journey of self-discovery and had taught her the importance of confronting the darkness within. The whispers in the night had become a reminder of her own strength and the connection she had forged with the spirits of the eternal house.

From that day forward, Sarah lived her life with a newfound appreciation for the unknown. She embraced the whispers in the night, knowing that they held the secrets of a world beyond our own. And as she continued to explore the mysteries of the supernatural, she carried the lessons learned from the eternal house and the painting that had brought her face to face with the spirits of the past.

## Chapter 2
# Interview: The Paranormal Investigator

In this interview, we sit down with Mark Thompson, a seasoned paranormal investigator who has dedicated his life to uncovering the truth behind haunted locations. Mark shares his experiences investigating the eternal house, recounting the chilling encounters he and his team had with the trapped spirits. He provides insights into the supernatural phenomena they witnessed and the challenges they faced in their quest for answers.

As the sun began to set, casting an eerie glow over the room, I sat down with Mark Thompson, a renowned paranormal investigator who had dedicated his life to unraveling the mysteries of the supernatural. With a calm demeanour and a glint of excitement in his eyes, Mark began to recount his experiences investigating the infamous eternal house.

"It all started with rumours," Mark began, leaning forward in his chair. "Whispers of a house that was plagued by restless spirits, trapped in a never-ending cycle of torment. The eternal house had gained a reputation for being one of the most haunted locations in the country, and my team and I were determined to uncover the truth."

Mark's team consisted of seasoned investigators, each with their own unique set of skills and expertise. Armed with an array of high-tech equipment and a deep understanding of the paranormal, they embarked on their journey into the heart of darkness.

"The first time we stepped foot inside the eternal house, we could feel the weight of its history," Mark recalled, his voice tinged with a mix of excitement and trepidation. "The air was heavy, and an unsettling silence hung in the air. It was as if the house itself was holding its breath, waiting to reveal its secrets."

As they began their investigation, Mark and his team encountered a myriad of supernatural phenomena. They witnessed objects moving on their own, disembodied voices echoing through the halls, and chilling apparitions that seemed to materialize out of thin air.

"One of the most chilling encounters we had was in the attic," Mark shared, his voice dropping to a hushed tone. "We heard the sound of children laughing, but there were no children present. It sent shivers down our spines, knowing that the spirits of innocent souls were trapped within those walls."

But it wasn't just the apparitions and strange sounds that made the eternal house a daunting place to investigate. Mark and his team faced numerous challenges along the way.

"The energy within the house was incredibly intense," Mark explained. "It drained us both physically and emotionally. We had to constantly remind ourselves to stay grounded and focused, even in the face of fear and uncertainty."

Despite the challenges, Mark and his team pressed on, determined to bring peace to the trapped spirits and shed light on the dark history of the eternal house. They conducted extensive research, delving into the house's past and consulting with experts in the field of paranormal activity.

"Our goal was not just to document the supernatural occurrences but to understand the reasons behind them," Mark emphasized. "We wanted to give a voice to the spirits, to acknowledge their pain and suffering, and hopefully, help them find peace."

As the investigation progressed, Mark and his team made significant breakthroughs. They discovered that the eternal house had a long history of tragedy and despair, with each event leaving an indelible mark on the spirits that lingered within its walls.

"We conducted séances and communicated with the spirits, offering them a chance to share their stories," Mark revealed. "Through these interactions, we were able to piece together the puzzle of their existence and provide them with the closure they desperately sought."

After months of tireless investigation, Mark and his team finally achieved their goal. The eternal house, once a place of darkness and despair, became a beacon of hope and redemption. The trapped spirits found solace, and the house itself seemed to breathe a sigh of relief.

As our interview came to a close, I couldn't help but feel a sense of awe and admiration for Mark and his team. Their dedication to uncovering the truth and bringing peace to the spirits was truly remarkable.

As I left the interview, the stories of the eternal house and Mark's experiences lingered in my mind. They served as a reminder that there is still so much we don't understand about the supernatural world, and that there are individuals like Mark who are willing to venture into the unknown to seek answers.

And as I walked away, I couldn't help but wonder what other mysteries awaited us, just beyond the veil of our everyday reality.

Chapter 3

# Short Story: "The Lost Journal"

In this short story, we stumble upon an old journal hidden within the walls of the eternal house. The journal belongs to a previous owner, who documented their descent into madness as the house's haunting grip tightened. Through the pages, we witness their unraveling sanity and the desperate attempts to escape the clutches of the eternal house. Will the journal provide any clues to the secrets that lie within?

Deep within the decaying walls of the eternal house, a forgotten secret lay hidden, waiting to be discovered. It was a lost journal, belonging to a previous owner who had fallen victim to the house's malevolent grip. As fate would have it, I stumbled upon this journal, unlocking a haunting tale of madness and despair.

The journal's pages were yellowed with age, the ink faded but still legible. It belonged to a man named Samuel, who had once called the eternal house his home. As I began to read his entries, I was immediately drawn into his descent into darkness.

Samuel's first entries were filled with excitement and hope. He described the grandeur of the eternal house, its ornate architecture, and the promise of a new beginning. But as the days turned into weeks, his tone shifted, and a sense of unease crept into his words.

Strange occurrences plagued Samuel's days and nights. He wrote of whispers in the dark, shadows that danced along the walls, and a constant feeling of being watched. His once steady hand now trembled as he chronicled his growing paranoia and the toll it took on his sanity.

As I turned the pages, Samuel's entries became more erratic and disjointed. His words were filled with fear and desperation, as if he was fighting a losing battle against an unseen force. He wrote of doors slamming shut on their own, objects moving without explanation, and the feeling of icy fingers brushing against his skin.

In one chilling entry, Samuel described a night of terror that would forever haunt him. He wrote of waking up to find himself trapped in his own bedroom, the walls closing in around him. The air grew thick with an otherworldly presence, suffocating him with its malevolence. Samuel's pleas for help went unanswered, as if the house itself reveled in his torment.

As I read on, it became clear that Samuel's grip on reality was slipping. His entries became a jumble of fragmented thoughts and incoherent ramblings. He wrote of figures lurking in the shadows, whispering secrets that only he could hear. The eternal house had claimed his mind, trapping him in a never-ending nightmare.

But amidst the chaos, there were glimmers of hope. Samuel wrote of his desperate attempts to escape the clutches of the eternal house. He sought the help of priests, mediums, and even attempted to perform his own rituals to banish the spirits that tormented him. But each attempt proved futile, as the house's grip only tightened.

The final entry in the journal was a plea for someone to find his words, to uncover the truth behind the eternal house's haunting. Samuel's last words were filled with resignation and a sense of impending doom. He knew that his fate was sealed, but he hoped that his journal would serve as a warning to others who dared to enter the eternal house.

As I closed the journal, a chill ran down my spine. Samuel's story had left an indelible mark on my soul. The lost journal had provided a glimpse into the darkness that lurked within the eternal house, a darkness that claimed the sanity and lives of those who dared to call it home.

I couldn't help but wonder if there were others like Samuel, lost souls trapped within the eternal house's walls. And as I left the house, the weight of its secrets heavy on my shoulders, I vowed to share Samuel's story, to shed light on the haunting that had plagued the eternal house for centuries.

Chapter 4
# Interview: The Local Historian

In this interview, we speak with Emma Johnson, a local historian who has dedicated her life to uncovering the history of the eternal house. Emma shares her research findings, shedding light on the dark past of the property and the tragic events that led to its haunting. She discusses the impact the house has had on the town and the lingering fear that still permeates the community.

In the heart of the town, I sat down with Emma Johnson, a local historian who had dedicated her life to unraveling the dark history of the eternal house. With a stack of old documents and photographs before her, Emma began to share her research findings, shedding light on the tragic events that had led to the house's haunting.

"The eternal house has a long and troubled past," Emma began, her voice filled with a mix of fascination and trepidation. "It was built in the late 1800s by a wealthy family, the Harringtons. They were known for their opulent lifestyle and extravagant parties."

As Emma delved deeper into her research, she discovered that beneath the surface of grandeur, the Harrington family harboured dark secrets. The patriarch, Jonathan Harrington, was rumoured to have made a pact with dark forces in exchange for wealth and power.

"The Harringtons' prosperity came at a great cost," Emma explained. "The house became a breeding ground for tragedy and despair. Unexplained deaths, mysterious disappearances, and a general sense of unease plagued the family and those who entered the house."

Emma's research revealed a series of tragic events that unfolded within the eternal house. She spoke of a young girl who vanished without a trace, a maid who was found dead under mysterious circumstances, and a family member who was driven to madness.

"These events left an indelible mark on the house," Emma continued. "The spirits of those who suffered within its walls remained trapped, their restless souls haunting the eternal house to this day."

As we discussed the impact of the eternal house on the town, Emma revealed that the haunting had permeated the community, leaving a lingering fear in its wake. People spoke in hushed whispers about the house's dark history, and many avoided passing by it after dark.

"The eternal house has become a cautionary tale," Emma said. "It serves as a reminder of the consequences of delving into the supernatural and the dangers of making pacts with the unknown," Emma said with a somber tone.

"The eternal house stands as a cautionary tale, a chilling reminder of the consequences that await those who dare to delve into the supernatural realm and make deals with forces beyond their comprehension. Its haunted halls and restless spirits serve as a stark warning, a reminder that some secrets are better left untouched. The stories of John and Emily's harrowing journey within the eternal house will forever echo as a reminder of the dangers that lie in wait for those who seek to unlock the mysteries of the supernatural world. It is a chilling testament to the fragility of human curiosity and the price one may pay for venturing too far into the realm of the unknown."

# Reader Interaction

Dear readers,

As we reach the final chapter of "The Eternal House," I want to take a moment to express my gratitude for joining me on this haunting journey. Your support and engagement have meant the world to me, and I am thrilled to invite you to participate in the reader interaction section of this book.

"The Eternal House" is a story that explores the supernatural, delving into the depths of fear, redemption, and the consequences of our actions. It is my hope that this tale has sparked your imagination and perhaps even stirred memories of your own supernatural experiences.

I invite you to share your own stories, whether they be encounters with the paranormal, unexplained phenomena, or theories about the eternal house. Your experiences and insights are valuable, and by sharing them, we can create a community of readers who have been touched by the mysteries of the supernatural.

If you have a story or theory you would like to share, please reach out to me through the contact information provided below. I would love to hear from you and discuss your experiences. Your contributions may even be featured in future editions or discussions surrounding "The Eternal House."

**Contact Information:**
**- Email: wendysheffield@yahoo.co.uk**
**- Website: www.healingwithspirit.co.uk**
**- Social Media: Find me on Twitter, Facebook, and Instagram**

I believe that the power of storytelling extends beyond the pages of a book. It is through our shared experiences and conversations that we can deepen our understanding of the supernatural and its impact on our lives. Your stories and theories have the potential to inspire and captivate others, just as "The Eternal House" has captivated you.

Thank you once again for embarking on this journey with me. I look forward to hearing from you and continuing the exploration of the supernatural together.

With warm regards,

Wendy

# Author's Note

Hello" dear readers,

The Eternal House" was inspired by a fascination with the supernatural and a desire to explore the themes of sacrifice, redemption, and the consequences of our actions. It is a tale that delves into the darkest corners of the human psyche, where fear and courage collide, and where the power of love and empathy can triumph over even the most malevolent forces.

Throughout the narrative, John and Emily's journey serves as a metaphor for the struggles we all face in life. Their harrowing experience within the eternal house represents the trials and tribulations that can haunt us, trapping us in cycles of pain and despair. But it is through their sacrifice and willingness to confront their own demons that they find redemption and ultimately break free from the house's grip.

In writing this story, I wanted to encourage readers to contemplate the consequences of their actions and the power of redemption. We all make choices that have far-reaching effects, and it is important to recognize the impact we have on others and the world around us. The eternal house serves as a reminder that our actions, both good and bad, can have lasting consequences, and that it is never too late to seek redemption and find a path towards healing.

I hope that "The Eternal House" has sparked a sense of introspection within you, dear reader. May it serve as a reminder that even in the face of darkness, there is always hope. May it inspire you to examine your own actions and the choices you make, and to strive for empathy, forgiveness, and redemption.

As you close the final chapter of this story, I encourage you to carry its themes with you. Remember the power of sacrifice, the strength of love, and the importance of seeking redemption. And may you find solace in the knowledge that no matter how haunted our past may be, there is always the potential for a brighter future.

Thank you for joining me on this journey through "The Eternal House." May its lessons resonate within you long after you have turned the final page.

Wendy

Printed in Great Britain
by Amazon

42081502R00055